All About Rocks

by Cynthia Benjamin

PHOTOGRAPHY CREDITS: COVER ©Houghton Mifflin Harcourt; 4 (tl) ©Getty Images/Photodisc; 5 (bl) ©Ken Samuelsen/Getty Images; 5 (br) ©Stockbyte/Getty Images; 9 (b) ©Alan Curtis/Alamy Images; 9 (tr) ©J.D. Dallet/age fotostock/Getty Images; 10 (cr) ©RF Company/Alamy Images; 10 (bl) © tarajane/Fotolia

If you have received these materials as examination copies free of charge, Houghton Mifflin Harcourt Publishing Company retains title to the materials and they may not be resold. Resale of examination copies is strictly prohibited.

Possession of this publication in print format does not entitle users to convert this publication, or any portion of it, into electronic format.

Copyright © by Houghton Mifflin Harcourt Publishing Company

All rights reserved. No part of this work may be reproduced or transmitted in any form or by any means, electronic or mechanical, including photocopying or recording, or by any information storage and retrieval system, without the prior written permission of the copyright owner unless such copying is expressly permitted by federal copyright law. Requests for permission to make copies of any part of the work should be addressed to Houghton Mifflin Harcourt Publishing Company, Attn: Contracts, Copyrights, and Licensing, 9400 Southpark Center Loop, Orlando, Florida 32819-8647.

Printed in Mexico

ISBN: 978-0-544-07262-6

3 4 5 6 7 8 9 10 0908 21 20 19 18 17 16 15 14 13

4500456317   A B C D E F G

Contents

Introduction 3
Flint 4
Slate 5
Granite 6
Gold 8
Marble 10
Responding 12

Vocabulary
natural resource
rock
weathering

Stretch Vocabulary
mineral
slab
igneous
deposit
ore

Introduction

Which natural resource do people use to make houses, jewelry, and blackboards? The answer is rock.

A rock is a hard, nonliving object from the ground. Rocks are made of different minerals. Rocks have different colors and textures, depending on what they are made of and how they formed.

If you think rocks are useless, you may be surprised by all the things people do with rocks.

Geologists are scientists who study rocks.

Flint

These arrowheads were made with flint.

Flint is a hard rock made of a mineral called quartz. Flint comes in many colors.

Flint is easy to chip off in flakes. During the Stone Age, people made sharp tools and weapons from flint. They carved flint into knives and spears.

People have also used crushed flint to make sandpaper. Carpenters used the rough paper to make wood smooth.

Slate

Slate is a fine-grained, smooth rock. It is easy to split slate into thin pieces called slabs. These slabs are very strong, and they last a long time.

Slate comes in many different colors. Slate can be black, gray, red, green, brown, purple, or even spotted. The color depends on the minerals in the rock. The main minerals in slate are mica and quartz.

Sometimes roofs are made out of slate. Slate is good for roofing because it can be made into tiles that can last a long time in rain, snow, and wind.

Slate

School blackboards used to be made of slate.

Granite

A large part of every continent on Earth is granite. This hard rock has a rough grain. The minerals in granite give this rock a white, pink, or light gray color. Most granites are speckled with different colors.

Granite is an igneous rock. Granite forms when very hot, liquid rock, called magma, cools slowly deep underground. As it cools, it forms crystals of minerals like quartz, feldspar, and mica. Most of North America is made of granite buried under other rocks.

Wind and water can break down rock into small pieces. This process is called weathering. Granite does not break down quickly, though. Weathering of granite takes hundreds of years.

Because granite is so long-lasting, it is a great building material. Builders use granite on the outside of large buildings. Builders make the countertops in many houses with granite, too.

People use polished granite to build monuments and columns. The faces of four American presidents are carved into a granite mountain in South Dakota. This famous monument is Mount Rushmore.

Granite

Granite is sometimes used to cover kitchen countertops.

Gold

Gold is a shiny metal with a beautiful yellow color. Because it is soft, gold can be formed into different shapes without breaking. It does not rust like some other metals do.

Pure gold is rare and valuable. For thousands of years, people used gold as money. Since ancient times, people have made gold into jewelry. Olympic athletes compete to win the gold medal in their sports. Electronics companies use gold in radios, televisions, and computers. Heat, electricity, light, and sound can flow through gold easily.

Gold is in many rocks and in soil. Scientists at mining companies look for large amounts of gold. These are called gold deposits. Miners often find gold deposits in cracks in rock. A rock that contains metal, such as gold, is called ore.

This gold jewelry was made in ancient Egypt.

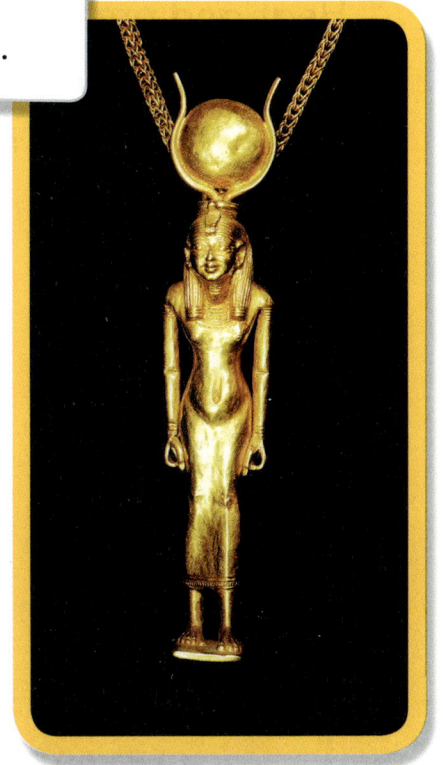

Some gold ore is near Earth's surface, but most gold ore is deep under the ground. To remove the gold ore, miners must drill and blast it out.

gold ore

Marble

Heat and pressure in Earth's crust form marble from limestone. When this happens, the limestone changes. The result is rock made up of large, rough grains of the mineral calcite.

Calcite marble

This statue was carved from marble.

The Lincoln Memorial, Washington, D.C.

If you look at marble under a microscope, you will see tiny cracks. These cracks make marble hard to remove without breaking it. Miners use machines to remove marble from the rock around it.

When marble forms, different minerals are made. Because of these minerals, marble comes in different colors. The purest marble is white. Some marble has a yellow, green, or reddish color.

Marble is a beautiful, strong rock. People use it for buildings, tile, and countertops. Marble is also fairly soft, which makes it easy for artists to carve into statues. But marble also weathers quickly. As a result, marble on buildings and monuments doesn't last as long as some other rocks, like granite.

Responding

Go on a Rock Hunt

Look for three or four different rocks. Find information on the Internet to help you identify the rocks you collect. Label and display each rock as part of a classroom project.

Write a Rock Guide

Write an entry for a rock guide. Describe the size, shape, color, and texture of the rock. Learn which minerals make up the rock. Then explain how people use the rock today. Discuss what you learned with your classmates.